VERY FAR AWAY

VERY FAR AWAY

BY MAURICE SENDAK

HARPER & BROTHERS, PUBLISHERS, NEW YORK

Very Far Away

Copyright © 1957 by Maurice Sendak
Printed in the United States of America
All rights in this book are reserved.
Library of Congress catalog card number: 57-5356

FOR **LOUISE HALSEY**

WHO HAS LOTS OF TIME FOR EVERYBODY

WHERE IS VERY FAR AWAY?

8

Martin asked his mother a question but she was busy washing the baby and didn't even hear him.

"So I'll go away," thought Martin. "Somewhere even very far away where somebody will answer my questions." And he packed his bag.

Then he put on a cowboy suit and a false mustache
—so no one would recognize him—

14

and went looking for very far away.

And on the way he met an old horse and an English
sparrow who were having a very serious discussion.
"Where is very far away?" asked Martin.
"Because that is where I want to go."

"Very far away is where people are refined," said the sparrow. "Like the place where I was born." And she began to cry.

"Very far away is where a horse can dream," said the horse. "The way I used to dream in the deep blue grass and—" He began to cry.

"Why are you crying?" asked Martin.
"Because," said the sparrow and the horse, "very
far away is where we' want to be!"
"I know just what you mean," said Martin
and he began to cry too.
"Hello," said somebody.

"Oh," cried the sparrow. "A cat!" And she flew up on Martin's hat.

"Don't be afraid," said the cat. "Why are you crying? What's the matter?"

"We want to go very far away," said Martin, "and we don't know how to get there."

"I know just what you mean," said the cat. "Very far away is where a cat can sing all day, and nobody says, *hush cat!*"

"And where somebody answers my questions!" shouted Martin.

"—Where horses dream," said the horse.

"—And people are refined," said the sparrow.

"I know a place very far away," said the cat.

"Where?" asked Martin.

"Many times around the block and two cellar windows from the corner," answered the cat.

"Want to go?"

"*Yes!*" they all shouted. So they did. And when
they came to the place that was very far away
Martin said, "Oh how happy we'll be."

"Forever," said the horse.

"—And ever," sighed the sparrow.

And they climbed through the window one by
one, except the horse. He stuck in the middle
with his head on the inside and the rest of him
on the outside.

VERY FAR AWAY

34

Martin took off his cowboy hat and began asking questions and everybody had time to answer.

The sparrow told them about the place where she was born. How refined the people were and how she ate crumbs from the king's plate.

And the horse had a dream. He dreamt he jumped over an apple tree. He dreamt he lay in deep blue grass and it covered him like a blanket.

And the cat sang a happy song about sunshine and a kitten playing with his mother's tail. And a sad song about moonlight and an empty tin can. They lived together very happily for an hour and a half.

Then the cat said to Martin, "You ask so many questions, I can't hear myself sing." "Then stop singing," said Martin. "And just answer my questions."

"Stop talking," said the horse sleepily. "Very far away is where a horse can dream of long ago and not be disturbed by the usual noise."

"No, no," said the sparrow politely. "Very far away is where people are refined and do not raise their voices."

"I didn't go very far away to watch horses dreaming dreams!" shouted the cat. "Or hear refined stories about old crumbs and kings!"

"And *nobody* answered my last question!" said Martin.

"You ask too many!" screeched the cat.

"You sing too loud!" shouted Martin.

"No one listens to me at all!" cried the sparrow.

"I'm going home," said the horse.

And he did.

"Well," said the sparrow, "if this is very far away it isn't far away enough for me." And she flew out the window.

"I'll go find a new very far away place," said the cat. "And I'll never never invite anybody again." And she stalked out the window.

Martin was left all by himself.

"Maybe the baby's all washed," he thought. He put on his cowboy hat.

"But if Mama's *still* not finished I'll sit on the steps and count automobiles while I wait."

He picked up his bag and climbed out the window.

"And then Mama will tell me what refined means and why horses dream and why cats ever sing when they don't know how."

Martin ran all the way home.